HEED

HEED
Fragrance of Freedom

CASSANDRA SZAFRANSKI

PALMETTO
PUBLISHING
Charleston, SC
www.PalmettoPublishing.com

Copyright © 2024 by Cassandra Szafranski

All rights reserved

No portion of this book may be reproduced, stored in a retrieval system, or transmitted in any form by any means—electronic, mechanical, photocopy, recording, or other—except for brief quotations in printed reviews, without prior permission of the author.

Paperback ISBN: 979-8-8229-5654-3

DEDICATION

This brief is dedicated to my children. My greatest wish is that when you look back on our journey, you see God's grace, love, protection, and PLAN for us. Through all my failures, He was faithful and fought for us to enjoy the fragrance of freedom. Heed, sweet boys, His love is greater.

INTRODUCTION

Heed: *To pay close attention to;*

Walking up to the church through clouds of cigarette smoke, I focused on one step in front of the other lest I turn around and leave. I made this walk every Monday night to attend my weekly meeting and promptly found my regular seat on the right side of the circle. Routinely, I introduced myself before sharing my input on the topic, "Hi, my name is Cassandra and I am an addict". I have presented my testimony for several women's groups and always began with, "My name is Cassandra and I was once a victim of domestic violence".

These opportunities provided growth and support for me that I will always treasure. However, today, it is with immeasurable gratitude I am able to introduce myself to you without attachment. Hello reader, my name is Cassandra. I have many parts to my story but they are not my identity.

This brief is an introduction to an initiative started to cultivate conversation and attentiveness to the aromas of life. All names have been changed and many details omitted for the privacy, safety and respect for the characters in this memoir.

Blueberry Muffins

My legs swing, hanging from the counter stool. Set up with a collection of homemade paper dolls and a milk jug school, I (somewhat) patiently await my grandmother's mini blueberry muffins. This was *our* special thing. The scent of the oven filled the house with a sweet, blueberry smell that felt like her warm hugs. We sang songs and played, sun beaming through the bay window. Together with her is the sweetest aroma. A safety, understanding, love, empowerment, and joy that I felt particularly with her. Life is as simple and sweet as the aroma of her mini blueberry muffins.

Dandelions and Wheelbarrows

It tickles my nose as I brush through the dandelion patch in search of slugs. I have a collection going in the wheelbarrow on the opposite side of the yard. At this point, I have picked through each blade of fresh, green grass and dandelion. I have turned over every rock. I am certain I have collected all the slugs inhabiting the yard stretching nearly an acre. This is an all day event- an event I attend often. The summer air enters my nose and fills my lungs in one deep breath. Life is as beautiful and warm as the aroma of a summer afternoon.

Snickerdoodles

Christmas season means a harmony of saccharine cookies. Snickerdoodles are mom's specialty. Warmed by the fire with my baby doll in tow, I work my way to the kitchen to lick the spoon. This is the best part. I slide on the mitt, far too big for my hand, and turn with a grin waiting for the spoon. I can smell the cinnamon before the spoon even touches my lips. It is the smell of "home for the holidays", snow days, and board games by the fire. Life is as home-y as cinnamon and sugar on a spoon.

My Great's Perfume

Great, as I endearingly call her, is starting to act... different. She gets angry sometimes- completely out of character. She forgets words often and needs help using the restroom. Mom says her brain is changing and it is not something I am old enough to understand- dementia. I see my Great every day. She combs my hair, and we eat lunch together while we watch the birds. My Great is changing. Sometimes she forgets who I am now. When she sits next to me, the one thing that has not changed is the smell of the perfume on her handkerchief. I look over at her crocheting intricate doilies. She is so beautiful. I wonder, does the smell of my shampoo remind her I am her Cassandra? Life is as nostalgic as my Great's perfumed handkerchief.

Musty School

High school is tough for everyone, right? Pushing through the double wide doors, I enter the old, musty building with purse in hand. This is high school- everyone uses a purse now. My first stop is to the restroom. Hands against the cold porcelain sink, I lean into the mirror. *"Please God, let today be a better day"*. It was not. I feel so misunderstood-displaced. I am so alone. Nobody can hear my silent cries as I push the double wide doors open with the decrepit building smell stuck to my uniform shirt. Tears roll down quicker as I walk down the sidewalk and take the first step onto the bus. Life is as persistently brutal as my high school bully.

The Uniform Store

My low self-esteem does not allow me to make eye contact much. As I gaze left, right, and occasionally up, I notice name brand shoes and women with expensive handbags. The smiles I catch are gentle. It smells like redolent perfumes and price tags. We are here to find uniform attire for my new school. The woman fitting me touches my shoulder, as I had clearly lost attention. I look up to the mirror and smile. This is my new, fresh start. Yes, life is as empowering as the aroma of the uniform store.

Plastic Bins and Car Rides

The ride is a mixture of tears and laughter. I am on my way to college now. I earned a scholarship, gained some confidence, and have an army of support by my side-including my parents and the man I surely will marry. What else could I possibly wish for? The car is packed tightly. The scent of plastic bins, dorm room plants, and sunlight surround my face nearly touching the window. My heart is full of joy, excitement, and mere disbelief. I am at this phase in life now. It is a bewilderment of emotion. Life is as ambitious and mystifying as the car ride to college with the greatest support in my life.

Apples

The night air is crisp, and the sky is cloudy, hiding the moonlight. I pack an apple with marijuana and take the first inhale. Blowing out the air into a toilet paper roll spoof, I can smell the dryer sheet and smoke mixture. I do not feel any different like my friends said I would. A few inhales later I find myself giggling at nothing- now I understand. This is my first experience getting high. The following several years will be filled daily with similar experiences- I was hooked, but it wasn't enough to find fullness in my empty body. Life is as fragrant as the spoof toilet paper roll- diluted, misleading, lost.

White Roses

One time he picked through a share size bag of skittles, removing the purple ones. I hate purple skittles, so this gift made for a very thoughtful Monday morning. I drive fifteen minutes to his college and knock on the dorm room door. He meets me at the door with a white rose in hand- my favorite. White roses seem to be more fragrant. They are pure, blameless, simple, and still so strikingly beautiful and resilient. This time is different when I look at the man I came to college with, once full of love. This time, I feel nothing at all. I am completely numbed by my behavior and spend the afternoon short and reserved. Life is as bitter as choosing drugs over the aroma of the purist, white rose.

Trap House

The music vibrates my soul as I walk up the steps. My hands are shaking, and I am sweating. I open the door to a house full of other shaking, sweaty people- but they have smiles. I pour myself a glass of hard liquor as the homeowner walks by and drops a few rocks of MDMA in my cup. The smell of the whiskey overtakes the smell of sweat, and my hands stop shaking when I see the rocks splash. My body can function again, but I am not euphoric, so I accept the invitation for more and make my way to the bathroom. There, on the bathroom sink, is a line waiting for me- but it doesn't look like my usual. Ketamine. Surely, this will satisfy the craving to get high. My nose nears the bathroom sink, this time it is not to notice a fragrance of any sort, rather, to avoid noticing anything else in the way life is going. It goes down easy. So do I. My palms hit the short span of the wall between the sink and toilet and my body sinks to the floor. I presume I am here for some time. When I get back up, it is morning. The time between is lost completely and I make my way to leave. The traffic lights on the way home dance just as the lights of the trap house did. My body hurts. Life is as fragrant (or not) as we choose it to be. I choose anosmia.

Salt Water and Jet Skis

My shoulders are warmed by the sun as the cool water splashes my legs. The jet ski glides through the water effortlessly, fast, turning and spewing water so loud I can barely hear my own laughter. I am on a trip with my friends with beautiful scenery that we enjoy between sessions of getting high. We are pretty far out in the water and my body begins to hurt- it is about that time. Turning around the jet ski, I feel lightheaded. I need to get back- fast. I feel relief pulling up to the dock. Opening my purse, I sort through what I have. It is a mad scientist cocktail now to maintain functionality. Anything I do not need to insert into my veins, I will ingest to feel "normal". Life seems permanently dependent on poor choices, as salty as the water that day. Even I know I am too far down the wrong path now.

The Lights

My jaw hurts. I can feel my teeth gnashing together but I cannot stop. The aroma here is free spirited, love, and bright. The lights are flashing, people are dancing, and I am standing by the bathroom door with my arms folded and jaw locked shut. The rave scene is my newest endeavor. It is the perfect place for MDMA, which around here is cut primarily with meth. I am hooked. I can feel the DJ set start to change through the soles of my feet, up my body, and straight to my jaw. My eyes are fixed on the dancing, gloved hands of a fellow festival attendee. Suddenly, the dancer disappears but my gaze remains fixed. A security guard approaches with a gentle touch on the shoulder to make sure I am okay. "I am" I reply, almost in a whisper. On the surface, life is captivating and adventurous. Life is the aroma of a careless free spirit. Oh, naivety.

Breakfast Sandwiches

The night is a blur. My dad drove an hour searching the city for me with no inclination to where I was. He found me in the back seat of my car and dropped me off. The next thing I remember is it is two in the morning. It is raining and I am walking the sidewalks with a friend. Lost. *Who can I call at this hour? Not my dad again.* I call him. The man I had broken months before, the man I had everything with that I willingly gave up for...this. He answers and promptly shows up at the road crossing per my description. I hop in the truck, friend in tow, and am met with the smell of breakfast sandwiches and coffee. The ride back is a silent one. Not one word is spoken. He hands us the sandwiches and fresh coffee and tells me to stay safe, tears in his eyes. "Thanks," I said it so quietly I am not sure he even heard, and I was gone again. Life is as forgetful and heartless as my actions to those I love and loved me unconditionally.

A Grandmother's Doiley

I wish I could say we are here for a thoughtful visit to a caring grandmother. Pulling the dining chair, I take a seat next to the unwitting woman and begin to create small talk. Every now and again I glance up at the sound of cupboards opening and closing behind her as he rummages through for pill bottles. My hands tremble nearly as much as my nervous thoughts. I am disgusted with myself. My heart is broken for this woman, but, addiction calls. I glance back down at the table. Laying dead center, hosting a beautiful vase of flowers, is a doily. I tear up, thinking of my Great. With the conversation cut short, I suddenly stand up and we say a quick goodbye, pockets full. On the way out the door, I smell my Greats perfume as if she were there with me. The tears stream down my cheeks, but my hands are calm. I know he loves his grandmother too, just as I love my Great. Life is as conflicting as knowing what is right and doing what is wrong anyhow.

The Psych Ward

It smells like a hospital. It smells like state grade hand sanitizer, hopelessness, and a hint of cranberry juice. It smells like plain, white walls. I am surrounded by homeless individuals lining benches outside rooms because there is no more space. The consistent beeping of hospital signals ring in my ears. I am desperate. The wait list for help is long and I am certain I will be dead by the time I get a chance to plead my case for help. My mom has spent many sleepless nights in prayer, trying to pull any professional connections, desperate to save me. I am convinced I cannot be saved. Nobody knows the depths of my addiction. I hide it well- so I think. The depression that follows, however, is no longer able to be subdued. I am at my end. I am ready to die. I cannot continue this way and I cannot stop. Life is as inodorous as the plain, white walls of the psychiatric hospital.

My Childhood

I am home now- just for a short while. The aroma of snickerdoodles and candles is far from my memory. All I smell is smoke. Is it me? Has my childhood escaped me or has the home somehow morphed from what I reminisce? Life is... what is life anymore?

The Gas Mask

I seal the gas mask tight to my head, making sure it is airtight. I pack the marijuana and top it with my daily dose of cocaine. I light it with a deep inhale. The mask fills with the aroma of the "snow cone". Peace. I repeat the process several times with my morning cocktail. I honestly cannot recollect what the cocktail is this particular morning. My body feels okay again, and I begin to experience euphoria. The corner of my living room has an air freshener, set to release the fragrance of cinnamon apple every fifteen minutes to cover up the smell of breakfast. I hear the spray of the freshener and am filled with a sudden fear. I hide under the table and pull the closest blanket nearby. In anticipation, my eyes scan the room, looking for danger. It sprays again, sending my heart into a flutter like clockwork. Life is as frightening as the scent of cinnamon apple air freshener- oh, wait, never mind. I am in control.

The OBGYN

The office is quaint. My heart skips beat in excitement. This is surely the key to sobriety. I am in love. I eagerly tell the nurse as a naive nineteen years old that I am ready for motherhood. As we begin the procedure to remove my IUD birth control, the news came. I am already pregnant. Removal means termination. Life is as helpless as the aroma of lotion infused tissues at the OBGYN.

HOME

The nostalgic aroma of home again. I became pregnant quickly after my loss- it is go time. My blood pressure is a roller-coaster and I experience symptoms of withdrawal that are unbearable. The first several months of my pregnancy are a plethora of emotions ranging from anticipation to depression. Thank God for my support system. Mom walks up and offers a blanket before taking a seat across from me on the couch. Scrolling through images of what the nursery will be the nostalgic smell of home fills my head again. How will my sweet boy remember the fragrance of home?

The Hospital

The hospital replaces its plain, white walls with baby blue ones. The ringing of bells is constituted with a sweet lullaby. Malachi, your name derived from a dream. It is a biblical reference in remembrance of His word. No matter how far from God we feel, He is close, waiting for us to embrace the aroma of his sweet, loving grace and freedom. They place him on my chest. This must be the love I had always heard about in church. The smell of a newborn baby. The smell of a love I cannot begin to describe with words. The smell of second chances, new beginnings, newborn cries signifying life. Life is the aroma of new life. Life is as these distinctive, incredible aromas.

Coke

Relapse sucks. Relapse brings me to a place of forgetting the new life aroma. Relapse robs my innocent baby boy of a caring mother. Relapse is the smell of dirty diapers that do not fill my trash can, but the trash of someone able to care for my precious boy. I smell gasoline as my nose nears my kitchen counter. Fine white lines, perfectly distributed and a sink full of dirty dishes. I am incapable of being sorry. I am incapable of being anything but selfish. Life now is the aroma of selfish decisions and lack of the aroma of a nostalgic home for my boy.

Bloody Showers

I have been sober for some time now. I am grateful for my boy but there is something missing. Like a dry drunk, I live out my daily life miserable and making sure to share that misery with everyone I come in contact with. Surely, a baby will bring back the joyous aroma of the nostalgic home. Maybe it is lack of self-care, maybe it is a hereditary curse. Either way, my kidneys are going to be the death of me. I feel my second blessing squirm in my belly as I play with cars on the edge of the bathtub. The bathtub fills with blood. I cover with a towel as to not show my sweet Malachi the pain I am enduring. He is an intellectual child. He sleeps the nights with me on the floor of the bathroom, occasionally bringing glasses of ice when the nausea hits. These days are sad but rewarding. Together, we endure some of the most difficult challenges. Malachi, baby and I embrace the aroma of the difficulties of life- hope is on the horizon. Life is the fragrance of bloody bathtubs, awaiting promises, and laughter in play- even in the darkest moments.

Blue Walls

Titus, your name is a title of honor. Your name is a reminder of God's ultimate victory in our lives despite the devastation we have endured together. They place him on my chest and again the room seems to fill with the fragrance of new life. Relief runs through my veins. We made it. As I watch Malachi and Titus for the first time, my life feels complete. Life is the fragrance of new life and one of the strongest little boys I have ever encountered.

Disclaimer

Just as I have censored some of the darkest phases of my addiction, there are parts of my story that the delicacy of the law prohibits me from sharing fearlessly in the form of a short memoir. Instead, I have chosen to detail multiple forms of abuse and their signs. These are not all forms nor signs of abuse. If you or someone you know has or is experiencing abuse of any form, please see the "Resources" section at the end of this brief for help. Life is the fragrance of freedom so beautiful it fills the air around you.

Emotional Abuse

Emotional abuse smells like: name calling, controlling time/actions, dictating "rules", being made to feel unintelligent, your partner questioning your reality, abuser stating things didn't happen that did or vice versa (gaslighting), being critical of your appearance, jealousy over time spent with friends/family, monitoring/forcing to ask for permission, stalking, not allowing you to work, threats, or overloading with compliments/gifts as leverage (love bombing).

Physical Abuse

Physical abuse smells like: hair pulling, slapping, punching, kicking, physically restraining, or any other intentional, prevent you from eating, use of weapons against you, preventing you from contacting emergency services, harming children/pets, driving recklessly with you in the car, trapping you in your home, or any physical act that involved bodily contact.

Financial Abuse

Financial abuse smells like: providing an allowance and closely monitoring it, depositing your paycheck into an inaccessible account, preventing you from accessing accounts, limiting/preventing you from working, maxing out your credit cards or harming your credit score, stealing money from you or your family/friends, or refusing to provide money for necessary shared expenses.

Reactive Abuse

Reactive abuse smells like: manipulation. Reactive abuse is a tactic used to convince the victim or others that they are in fact the ones being abused. Victims may display behaviors in response to abuse that are not normal. This is categorized as reactive abuse.

Not A Victim

I shrink as if it were yesterday when I am labeled "victim". No, I am victorious. I am one of the blessed individuals who took the opportunity to leave an abusive situation. I am not a victim of domestic violence, I am Cassandra. I am a woman who chose new life. I am a woman who everyday enjoys the fragrance of freedom in a way I would not have experienced without my endeavors. I am blessed.

My Mother

I speak often of the fragrance of home. More specifically, this time, is the fragrance of my mother. I cannot imagine what she must be feeling. After coming to my rescue many times, she was still here. She welcomes me with open arms, and I can smell her beach vibe shampoo. She fills my cup, lets me know I am loved, supported, and never alone. She follows this with a harsh reality that I cannot allow the cycle to continue. I have two children whom I love dearly, and her words sink deep. I hear her tell me she cannot enable my decisions and tears well up in my eyes. If I could just be half the mother my mom is, my children can surely recover from this. We list my dreams and goals and begin to devise a game plan. I will regain my life again. I will regain a life my children deserve. This time, it is all on me. I have support but I must take the steps- I know she is serious. This is my turning point. We pray together and I smell the aroma of new life again- this time, it is mine.

Dry

I have been attending church again. I can feel God's grace doing work in me with each passing day. I still struggle with the aftermath of my life decisions, but He is so, so close. I attend meetings to maintain sobriety and begin planning the steps to rebuild. With two children and ten dollars to my name, I set off to smell the fragrance of freedom. Yes, even the thought of this scent overpowers every stenchy obstacle I will face in the following months. Life is the smell of dry drunk attitudes blossoming into a watered seed. With just a seed, I will grow a field of calming lavender, lilac, and all the beautiful things I missed over the years.

University

Life is the fragrance of bubble bath and fruit snacks bouncing along the path looking for my classes. It is the fragrance of family support as I plan my educational journey. It is the smell of lined paper, number two pencils, and dedication. This is the place I will grow over the next two years. I am here to finish my degree with dreams of contributing to the society I stole from and cheated during the years of my addiction. I am here to be the voice of those still in that place. I am here to give off the fragrance of freedom, new life, and the Creator who brought me redemption from the deepest pits. Lastly, I am here to enjoy the new fragrance with the two boys who help keep me grounded. I pray they too can enjoy the fragrance of hard work and freedom. It is a victimless walk down this path with my children. There are no more excuses and nobody to blame. This is a walk we will take together, rebuilding, dreaming, laughing, and *being*.

Matches

We sit on the steps of my new home. Torn down to the studs, as bare as my life had become, we rebuilt a beautiful place I can *feel* at home. I open my kitchen drawers and find there are no lighters. Instead, we have matches to light the candles. We have redolent baking cookies, citrus hand soaps at the sinks, and uncontainable joy. Life is the fragrance of the couch from the discount store, a closet stocked with diapers, and supernatural provision.

Inner City

My educational journey brought me to the inner city. It brought me to a place of injustices I had not experienced. It puts in perspective the immense opportunities I have been given to escape the harsh realities of my decisions. Coming from such a privileged background, these are struggles I could not have conceptualized. This brought another opportunity- one of remarkable gratitude. Never, should a person be bereaved of the opportunity to grow out of an obstructive situation. I want everyone to smell the fragrance of freedom- I am driven to break the chains of bondage in these communities and let the aroma fill the inner-city air.

Herbs

I no longer sleep on the bathroom floor. Instead, my room is flushed with herbs and plants. The humidifier and earthy aroma pervade the air. We use oils for everything. Every aliment, every sad day, every celebration, is met with a perfumery odor. It is a reminder of how each event is the scent I allow. Our Creator has endless fragrances to avail in, and I now purpose to stop and smell them all.

The Skydive

My adrenaline supersedes the nervousness. I launch and the air fills my nose and lungs as I let out a shout. Freefalling, every chain of destruction falling off in the open air. I can smell the fragrance of freedom in the altitudes of the clear skies. My arms spread out and I allow the wind to create enough resistance to enjoy the fall. The shoot comes out and I drift over my hometown. The aromas of burden relief, nostalgic homes, flowering fields, and pure love fill the entire sky, engulfing my body in an ineffable experience. Life is the scent of a free fall ten thousand feet up.

HEED

And so, it occurred to me that I not only want to fill my home, but the world with the fragrance of freedom. It is not only in my humble experience or in the confinements of an inner city that the scent is lost in the muddiness of life. I turn the knob on my stove to head the distiller and the calming, lavender hydrosol occupies my home. Heed Hydrosols is the initiative to share the aromas of freedom with the world. It is a gentle nudge out of complacency and into the awareness of our surroundings. Heed, readers, there is much to elate in, in this life and in the promise after. Life is as fragrant as what we heed to.

Graduation Day

Sometimes, I allow myself to benefit from the smell of the hope still to come. He has great plans for me, plans to prosper me. And this is the fragrance I imagine on graduation day. I imagine the blueberry muffins, dandelions, white roses, and new life. I imagine the fragrance of the bustling streets of the inner city. I imagine the blood bath replaced by a warm, lilac oil soak. I can smell the hope of a graduation gown packed in plastic. I can smell mud pie restaurants and children with the freedom to be children. Life is the fragrance of my Creator's mercy and love. Life is the fragrance of freedom. I choose mercy and love. I choose freedom.

RESOURCES

National Domestic Violence Hotline (800) 799-7233

The National Domestic Violence Hotline can be an ear to listen to or point you in the direction of proper resources in your area. They will ask if it is safe to talk and respect your privacy.

www.ingramcontent.com/pod-product-compliance
Lightning Source LLC
LaVergne TN
LVHW041716060526
838201LV00043B/766